I WANNA BE A DINOSAUR!

MATT HAUGEN AND STEPHANIE MIROCHA
ILLUSTRATED BY STEPHANIE MIROCHA
MUSIC BY MARTY HAUGEN

GIA Publications, Inc.
G-8582
ISBN: 978-1-57999-999-5

Published and distributed by GIA Publications, Inc.
7404 S. Mason Ave. , Chicago, IL 60638
www.giamusic.com

This book was printed October 2014 by R.R. Donnelley in Shenzhen, China.

“Mom, I’ve decided. I want to be a dinosaur!” said Carl.

“Me too! Me too!” said Sara.

“No! ‘Me Too’ is too young to be a dinosaur,” said Carl.

“Carl, your sister’s name is Sara, not ‘Me Too,’ ” said Mom, “and she can be a dinosaur if she wants. She’s almost three. That’s pretty old.”

"That's not old," said Carl.
"***Dimetrodon*** is old. He lived 300 million years ago and was even older than the dinosaurs. He was a giant proto-mammal, twice as long as me with a spiny sail on his back."

"I LOVE dinosaurs!" said Carl.

"What do you love?" asked Dad, joining the family for breakfast.

"Dinosaurs! I want to be a dinosaur, Dad," said Carl.

"Me too! Me too!" said Sara.

"*T. rex!* I'm king of the dinosaurs.

Tyrannosaurus rex!" roared Dad.

ROAR

"Big teeth, big claws, and a BIG appetite for tasty, tiny dinosaurs."

"Please roar quietly at breakfast," said Mom. "What kind of dinosaur should 'Me Too'—I mean, Sara—be?"

"A BIG one!" said Sara.

"She can be ***Diplodocus,*** " said Carl. "She would have 15 bones in her neck and 80 in her tail. She could c r a - - c k her tail like a whip! ***Diplodocus*** only ate plants and was still bigger than my school bus!"

"Bus! Bus! Me too," said Sara.

"No bus for Carl today," said Dad. "You and I are going to swimming lessons."

“It’s Saturday! Adventure day!” called Carl.

“Carl and I will be waiting for you two at the prehistoric playground,” said Mom.

"This pool is as warm as the Jurassic seas in the time of the dinosaurs," said Dad.

"Dinosaurs swim?" asked Sara.

"Dinosaurs were land animals, but there were also HUGE swimming reptiles," said Dad. "I'm a big, old ***Plesiosaurus*** with flippers that move me so fast any fish I see is lunch. Life sure is good at the top of the food chain!"

“You’ll never catch us, Mom,” called Carl.
“I’m not Mom…,” said Mom.

"I'm ***Allosaurus.*** I'm fast. I'm fierce.
I'm hungry.

I want some animals to snack on!"

"I'm not afraid of you!" cried Carl,

"I'm a dinosaur with serious
backbone—
mighty
Stegosaurus!"

"Watch out for my spiky tail.
I don't run. I just snack on
plants all day."

"There were even flying reptiles that lived with the dinosaurs," said Dad, "in all different sizes, some as big as a hang glider. Do you know what my favorite is called?

Pterodactylus!

I *soar* gracefully over the trees
I can

SWOOOP down
to catch a fish in
my strong jaws
before it even
sees me coming."

“We’ve already escaped from an allosaurus!” said Carl.
“I’m much ***f-a-s-t-e-r*** than an allosaurus,” said Dad.

"I'm ***Velociraptor!***
I'm small for a dino but quick and agile. And I've got a super special secret claw to grab you with. Plus, I look pretty cool with my colorful feathers."

"I think you've got a dinosaur-sized stomach," said Dad.
"You're quite the herbivore, Carl," said Mom.
"What's an herbivore?" asked Carl.
"An animal that eats only plants," replied Mom.

"Just like *Triceratops!*" said Carl. "He was big, bulky and built low to the ground for chewing up plants. Plus, he's got the triple horn threat."

Me too! Me too!

"Was *T. rex* really king of the dinosaurs?" asked Carl.

"No. Dinosaurs didn't have a king," said Dad. "*T. rex* wasn't even the biggest theropod around."

"What's a theropod?" asked Carl.

"Dinosaurs that walked on two legs were called theropods," said Mom. "They eventually evolved into birds. The BIGGEST was…***Spinosaurus!*** I've got the head of a crocodile and a fancy sail on my back. You'd better run if you see me!"

"I'd better be something really tough to survive you, *Spinosaurus!*" said Carl.

"I'm ***Ankylosaurus.*** I've got a spiky armor shell and I can whack anything with my super strong tail. I'm like a prehistoric super turtle."

"Sleep well, little Sara," said Mom.

"Dinosaur again. Big one. Big one," said Sara.

"You want to be one more, big dinosaur?" asked Dad.

"I know...," said Carl.

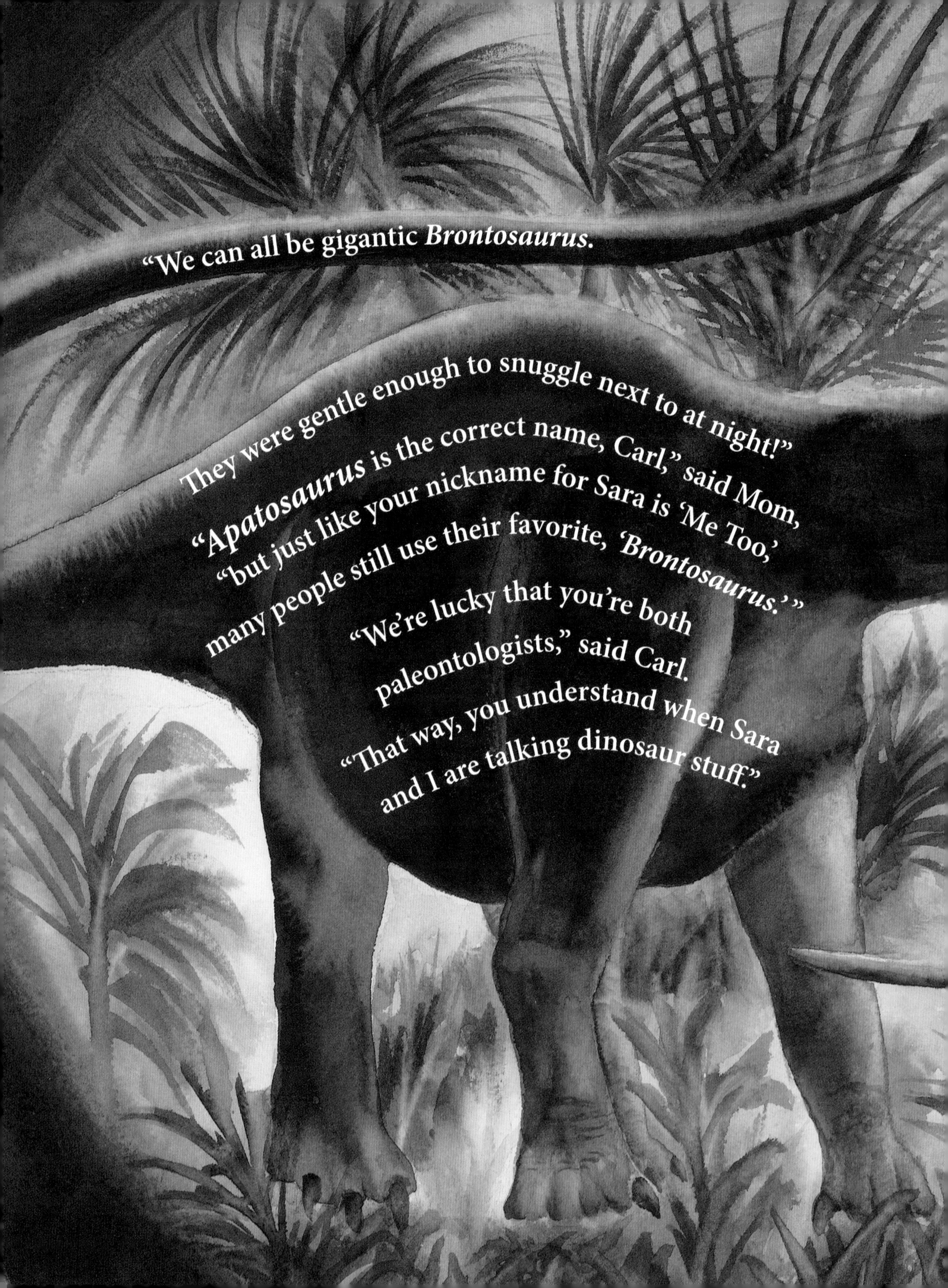

"We can all be gigantic *Brontosaurus*.

They were gentle enough to snuggle next to at night!"

"*Apatosaurus* is the correct name, Carl," said Mom,
"but just like your nickname for Sara is 'Me Too,'
many people still use their favorite, '*Brontosaurus*.' "

"We're lucky that you're both
paleontologists," said Carl.
"That way, you understand when Sara
and I are talking dinosaur stuff."

"Yup, we sure are lucky," said Dad.

"Sleep well, my little brontosaurs,"
whispered Mom.

Dimetrodon, a meat eater, lived millions of years before dinosaurs. It looked like some of the dinosaurs with its tall, spiny sail but was actually more closely related to the group of animals called mammals. By the time dinosaurs came along, *Dimetrodon* had disappeared, but some early mammals lived alongside the dinosaurs. No one knows for sure why *Dimetrodon* had a sail on its back. Maybe a sail made its back stronger, or helped *Dimetrodon* hide in tall reeds. Maybe the sail helped it to cool off and warm up or was good for attracting other dimetrodons. Why do you think *Dimetrodon* had its sail?

Tyrannosaurus rex is famous for appearing in movies as a big, fast, ferocious beast. Its mighty jaws had the strongest bite of any animal ever. *T. rex* could grow to about 40 feet long. Each year paleontologists discover new things about dinosaurs as they find more fossils, like puzzle pieces for a picture slowly getting put together. For example, a recent dig turned up a tyrannosaur fossil showing evidence of small feathers. It was not a *T. rex* fossil, but many paleontologists now wonder if *T. rex* might have looked a bit fluffy, too! *T. rex* used to be shown dragging its tail on the ground, but newer models show the tail held straight out behind to help *T. rex* balance. Scientists don't really know if *T. rex* actually ROARED—but it's fun to pretend it did! Perhaps one day you can become a paleontologist and make discoveries that change how we imagine our favorite dinosaurs.

Diplodocus was long, very long, growing close to 100 feet from the tip of its tail to its tiny head. *Diplodocus* may have been able to crack its tail like a whip to scare away predators, and each front foot had a big thumb claw. Every day *Diplodocus* lumbered about eating thousands of pounds of plants such as ferns, horsetails, pines, and gingko leaves. Look for gingko leaves on the page across from the school bus—and maybe also in your own neighborhood! The gingko trees we have today are the same species *Diplodocus* ate millions of years ago. Scientists think *Diplodocus* stripped leaves off plant stems with its peg-like front teeth and then, because it had no back teeth for chewing, swallowed the leaves whole—sort of like a plant vacuum cleaner! How long would it take you to eat a thousand pounds of plants?

Plesiosaurus was just one of many kinds of plesiosaurs that lived in ancient seas around the world for millions of years. It was one of the smaller ones, growing to about 9 to 16 feet long. The biggest ones were almost 50 feet long. All plesiosaurs had necks longer than their bodies, shorter tails, four flippers, strong jaws, and many teeth. They were at the top of their food chain, which means few or no other animals hunted them. Plesiosaurs didn't lay eggs like the dinosaurs. Instead, they gave birth to live baby plesiosaurs. Would you rather live on land or spend your life in the sea?

Allosaurus was a great hunter with sharp teeth and powerful legs. Its big, heavy tail helped to keep balance while walking. *Allosaurus* was a type of dinosaur called a theropod. Most theropods ate meat, walked on two legs, had short forearms, and had three main toes on their back feet. Theropods came in all sizes. *T. rex* was a theropod, bigger than *Allosaurus*, and lived millions of years later during the Cretaceous Period. Scientists think today's birds evolved from the smaller theropods. Can you think of any other dinosaurs that were theropods?

Stegosaurus is easily identified by the bony plates running down its back. Paleontologists think stegosaurs used those plates to attract mates rather than to fend off attacking dinosaurs. Hefty spikes on the ends of their powerful tails were good enough for that. Speaking of tails, horsetail is one of the plants

Permian Period

Triassic Period

Jurassic Period

290 million years ago

248

230

206

Age of Dinosaurs begins

Mammals

Sauropods

Stegosaurus might have eaten—an ancient (and nutritious) plant still around today. Look for horsetails next to *Stegosaurus*. Stegosaurs used their beaks to snap off food, and paleontologists believe they had a great sense of smell to help them find their favorite plants.

Pterodactylus had leathery wings stretched between arms and legs, and a short, fuzzy covering on its head and body that was neither exactly fur nor feathers. Paleontologists call this coating pycnofibres. 'Pterodactyl' is the name many people use when they're talking about *Pterodactylus*. Or sometimes they use it to mean the whole group of flying reptiles that lived during the time of dinosaurs. Paleontologists call this whole group pterosaurs. Pterosaurs came in all sizes. The smaller ones, like *Pterodactylus*, had a wingspan of about three feet. One of the largest was *Quetzalcoatlus* with a wingspan of about 35 feet!

Velociraptor, a theropod with feathers, was only about two and a half feet tall—not the scariest-looking dinosaur around! It did, however, have a special, sickle-shaped claw on each back foot for attacking small animals, and a jaw full of teeth for eating them. Paleontologists think *Velociraptor* may have been warm-blooded like today's birds. Do you see any other ways that today's birds are similar to ancient dinosaurs? Look on the *Velociraptor* page for buttercup flowers nodding their heads in the breeze, just like the plants *Velociraptor* saw millions of years ago.

Triceratops is easy to spot with its three horns and the frilly plate around its large head. *Triceratops* tromped around on stubby legs, grabbing ferns and other low-growing plants with its beak. Look behind *Triceratops* for the cycad tree. Cycads grew just about everywhere millions of years ago. *T. rex* lived alongside *Triceratops*, near the end of the Age of Dinosaurs. Scientists think debris and dust from a huge meteor hitting Earth changed the climate and made food hard to find, which led to a mass extinction of the dinosaurs. But not for all of them! Look outside at birds if you want to see some dinosaurs that are still with us!

Spinosaurus could grow to a whopping 55 feet long. Theropod meat eaters don't come any bigger than that! Like today's crocodiles, *Spinosaurus* lived both on land and in the water, and evolved to be excellent at catching fish. Spinosaurs had nostrils high up on the top of their snouts so they could lay low in the water, dip their jaws in and still breathe air. Paleontologists aren't sure why spinosaurs had sails on their backs. Maybe they waved their sails like colorful fans to attract mates. What do you think their sails were for?

Ankylosaurus, like *Stegosaurus*, had a very small brain compared to body size. Its skin was covered all over with bony plates, sort of like the skin of a crocodile or armadillo. With that kind of armor, it didn't need to outwit attackers. *Ankylosaurus* was big (25 to 30 feet long), heavy (about 13,000 pounds), and low to the ground. Weighing several tons, *Anklyosaurus* couldn't move very fast, but when fully grown was super protected. With one swing of its massive, club tail, *Ankylosaurus* could whack away a *T. rex!* Like all ankylosaurs, it was a plant eater with a beak for stripping off leaves.

Apatosaurus and *Brontosaurus* are different names for the same plant-eating animal. It was a sauropod, meaning a giant dinosaur that had a long neck, long tail, small head, thick body, and walked on four legs. Like all dinosaurs, *Apatosaurus* laid eggs. Its eggs were about the size of softballs. Baby *Apatosaurus* grew very quickly to get big before predators could catch and eat them. What colors were dinosaur skin, scales, knobs, plates, and feathers? Until scientists find out more, we'll just have to keep using our imaginations!

Jurassic Period

Cretaceous Period

144

65 million years ago

Mass Extinction

Ornithiscians

Theropods

Birds

Dedication

For Clio, my niece, and for dinosaur lovers everywhere. – S.M.

For Will, Everett, and Annie – Matt

Acknowledgements

Thank you to paleontologist Kristina Curry Rogers, Associate Professor in Biology and Geology at Macalester College, for her guidance in keeping us on track with dinosaur facts. Kristi discovered a dinosaur in Madagascar called *Rapetosaurus*. Look for its skull on top of the bookshelf page with the school bus!

Stephanie would also like to thank the Arrowhead Regional Arts Council (www.aracouncil.org) as a fiscal year 2014 recipient of a Career Development grant, which is funded in part with money from the Minnesota Arts and Cultural Heritage Fund as appropriated by the Minnesota State Legislature with money from the vote of the people of Minnesota on November 4, 2008; an appropriation from the Minnesota State Legislature; and the McKnight Foundation.

Marty would like to thank Stephanie and Matt for their patience and commitment in the efforts to make this book a reality.

Matt Haugen has written professionally as a journalist and in the nonprofit world. He's a graduate of Northwestern University and enjoys exercising his imagination muscles every day with his two sons.

Stephanie Mirocha is an award winning artist and published poet. Working mainly in watercolor media, she has illustrated three previous children's picture books portraying the beauty of earth's creatures. After extensive scientific research for each project, she adds a large measure of her love of nature to create imaginative, lifelike images. She is known for her playful use of design and bold colors. Look for lots of details on each page and a hidden picture hint revealing what comes on the next! Stephanie works out of her studio in Aitkin, Minnesota. To see more of her artwork visit her website at www.stephaniemirocha.com.

Marty Haugen is a composer with over 30 recordings, but this is his first experience of writing music for dinosaurs.

Readers can download a free mp3 containing songs recorded on Marty's *I Wanna Be a Dinosaur* CD and adapted to accompany the story at www.giamusic.com/dinosaur. The full recording is available from giamusic.com or any music vendor.